MIA MAYHEM

#13

AND THE WILD GARDEN

BY KARA WEST ILLUSTRATED BY LEEZA HERNANDEZ

LITTLE SIMON
New York London Toronto Sydney New Delhi

This book is a work of fiction. Any references to historical events, real people, or real places are used fictitiously. Other names, characters, places, and events are products of the author's imagination, and any resemblance to actual events or places or persons, living or dead, is entirely coincidental.

LITTLE SIMON
An imprint of Simon & Schuster Children's Publishing Division
1230 Avenue of the Americas, New York, New York 10020
First Little Simon hardcover edition June 2023

Also available in a Little Simon paperback edition

Designed by Chrisila Maida
Manufactured in the United States of America 0523 LAK
2 4 6 8 10 9 7 5 3 1
Library of Congress Cataloging-in-Publication Data
Names: West, Kara, author. | Hernandez, Leeza, illustrator.
Title: Mia Mayhem and the wild garden / by Kara West ; illustrated by Leeza Hernandez.
Description: First Little Simon paperback edition. | New York : Little Simon, 2023. | Series: Mia Mayhem ; 13 | Audience: Ages 5–9. | Summary: As part of her new mega-botany class at the Program for In-Training Superheroes, Mia Mayhem has to grow a plant from superseeds all on her own, but when her plant grows out of her control, she must find a way to stop the ensuing chaos.
Identifiers: LCCN 2022055324 (print) | LCCN 2022055325 (ebook) | ISBN 9781665917247 (paperback) | ISBN 9781665917254 (hardcover) | ISBN 9781665917261 (ebook)
Subjects: CYAC: Superheroes—Fiction. | Gardening—Fiction. | Schools—Fiction. | African Americans—Fiction. | LCGFT: Superhero fiction. | Novels.
Classification: LCC PZ7.1.W43684 Me 20223 (print) | LCC PZ7.1.W43684 (ebook) | DDC [Fic]—dc23
LC record available at https://lccn.loc.gov/2022055324
LC ebook record available at https://lccn.loc.gov/2022055325

CONTENTS

CHAPTER 1

ROSE VINE

BRRIINNGG!

Saved by the bell! My last class was finally over!

"Wanna walk home together?" asked Eddie Stein as we were leaving school.

"Sorry. I can't today," I told him. "I'm kind of in a rush."

"OH!" Eddie said with a wink. "Do you have a secret superhero mission?"

Now, you might think that Eddie was joking, but what he said was actually true.

My name's Mia Macarooney, and I. Am. A. Superhero. Like, for real!

Well, not right now.

At Normal Elementary School, I'm just a regular kid. But after school, I go to the Program for In Training Superheroes, aka the PITS.

The PITS is a top secret training academy where I learn all about my awesome superpowers. I even have a cool superhero name: Mia Mayhem.

Eddie is my best friend *and* the only one who knows my true superhero identity. Well, besides my parents . . . who are also superheroes.

It's a family thing.

But let's get back to the PITS, because I was starting a new superclass that day and didn't want to be late.

"See ya later, Eddie!" I called and sped off.

WHOOSH!

From the outside, the PITS looked like a boring, old, abandoned warehouse. You'd never guess that it was really a secret, high-tech superhero training academy.

At the entrance, I quick-changed into my supersuit. Then I shifted the crooked DO NOT ENTER sign, and a hidden screen popped up to scan my face. Time to go inside!

My classmates were already crowded into the lobby, which we called the Compass. Everyone was buzzing with excitement.

My friends Penn Powers and Allie Oomph waved for me to join them.

"How come we're meeting in the Compass?" I asked, confused.

Before Penn or Allie could answer, the whole class became quiet. Our headmistress, Dr. Sue Perb, walked into the Compass with a woman I'd never seen before.

"Hello, students!" Dr. Perb called. "I'm excited to announce our newest class here at the PITS: mega-botany! This class will be taught by Professor Rose Vine. Professor Vine was once

a student at the PITS, but she is now a famous professor of mega-botany. Normally, Professor Vine travels year-round to replant rain forests and collect seeds from the far reaches of the

earth. We are very lucky she agreed to teach this class. Welcome, Professor Vine!"

"Thank you, Dr. Perb," said Professor Vine. "I am so happy to be back at the PITS. Now, students, please follow me to the greenhouse."

The greenhouse?

Allie, Penn, and I all gave one another surprised looks. None of

us had ever been to the greenhouse before. The PITS was full of all kinds of secret places. Were we about to discover another one?

"What do you think is in the greenhouse?" I asked. "Maybe there will be a field of beautiful flowers, like the ones they carry in bouquets at weddings."

"Or maybe giant redwood trees," Allie said.

"What if there's a huge beanstalk that leads to a giant in the clouds?" Penn wondered.

I didn't know the answer, but there was only one way to find out. So we followed Professor Vine.

Mega-botany class was about to begin . . . and so was mega-trouble.

CHAPTER
2

The Greenhouse

Everyone gasped as we stepped inside the greenhouse. It was way cooler than we imagined.

It had both indoor and outdoor spaces, along with winding paths around a huge garden area.

There were beautiful, colorful flowers, plants, and trees in full bloom everywhere.

I wanted to explore everything, but Professor Vine called everyone over to a large fountain in the middle of a courtyard.

"It's time for your first assignment," she said. "You will each be growing your own plant using a botany kit."

Excited murmurs rippled through the greenhouse.

Professor Vine continued. "The purpose of this assignment is to learn

how to take care of plants, so that plants can take care of us."

A kid next to me raised their hand and asked, "How do plants take care of us?"

"Well, plants give us food and, most importantly, create the air we need to

breathe," Professor Vine answered.

Whoa! Plants do all *that*? I never knew plants were so cool. It's almost like they're superheroes too!

Next, Professor Vine showed us a botany kit, which came with a new flowerpot and a cool packet of superseeds.

"If you follow the instructions, everyone's plants should bloom over the next week," Professor Vine explained.

Then she passed out kits to each student . . . with vines that she launched out of her fingers!

Now that was seriously *awesome*!

"Please be very careful when you open your superseeds," Professor Vine warned. "These seeds are small, but they are also super.

So you do not want to lose them."

Now, the PITS is known for having the most amazing training classes ever, like flying, superspeed, X-ray vision, and more. So taking care of a plant seemed pretty easy. But knowing the PITS, nothing was ever easy.

I opened my botany kit. *That's strange.* My seed packet didn't have a label.

"Uh, Professor Vine?" I asked. "My seed packet is blank. How am I supposed to know what kind of plant I'm growing?"

"Great question," Professor Vine said. "The type of plant that blooms from your individual botany kits is meant to be a wonderful surprise for each of you. With that, please explore the rest of the greenhouse. Maybe you will find the plant that will sprout from your superseeds."

Our class split up as Professor Vine

walked around to tell us more about the plants in the greenhouse. I thought the medicinal herbs, which were plants that were grown and used for healing, were the coolest.

"I hope I have superlily seeds," said Allie. "What kind of plant do you think you'll grow, Mia?"

"Maybe a rose," I said, and took a big whiff of a nearby rosebush. "Roses smell so good."

"Nah, I bet your plant will be a cactus . . . or a Venus flytrap!" Penn joked.

Allie and I laughed, but then I started

thinking. Cacti were prickly, and Venus flytraps could be kind of scary. What if these superseeds were more dangerous than we thought?

Suddenly this assignment didn't seem so simple after all.

CHAPTER 3
MOM!
DAD!

CAT VS. SUPERSEEDS

"Mom! Dad! Check this out!" I called as soon as I got home from the PITS.

I headed straight to the kitchen to show my parents my awesome brand-new botany kit.

"I have to use this kit to grow a plant as part of our new mega-botany class," I explained. "And we don't know what kind of plant it is. It's a surprise!"

"How exciting!" Mom said. "That reminds me of our early superhero days, right after we graduated from the PITS. We had to battle a powerful plant villain, Evil Ivy, and her sticky sidekick, Thorn Wrecker."

"There were vines and thorns everywhere," Dad chimed in.

"That was one *creepy* battle. Get it? Like creeping vines? Anyway, can we help with your mystery plant?"

"Hmm, do we have any dirt I can use to plant my seeds?" I asked.

Luckily, Dad had some soil left over from our family garden in the backyard.

I took my botany kit outside. Chaos followed me. Chaos is my cat. You can probably tell by her name that wherever Chaos goes, disaster isn't far behind.

So with one eye on Chaos, I scooped some dirt into my flowerpot. Then I took the superseeds from my kit and carefully opened the packet. But just as

I was about to add them to the pot, Chaos jumped into my arms!

I caught the cat, but I dropped the superseeds! *Oh no!*

It was like slow motion as I watched the seeds fall through the air . . . and then they were *gone*!

I looked down and saw that they had all landed in my pot.

Phew! That was close.

"Please be more careful next time," I told Chaos.

Meow! Chaos flicked her tail and hopped out of my arms like nothing bad had happened.

That cat was full of close calls.

When I was sure Chaos was gone, I picked up the pot to move it where it would get the most sun. I knew the perfect place.

But then I tripped on a rock and . . . *SMASH!* The pot shattered, and my superseeds scattered everywhere!

My parents quickly came to help. Dad grabbed a new flowerpot from the shed, while Mom used her super-vision to help me find the superseeds in the dirt.

Then I replanted the seeds and watered them. Now all I had to do was wait for my mystery plant to grow.

SMASH!
BZZZZZZ!

CHAPTER
4

NORMAL PEOPLE PLANT PLANTS

I checked on my seeds the next morning. I wasn't sure what was supposed to happen, but all I saw was a plain old pile of dirt. Nothing had sprouted yet. *Ugh.*

At school, I told Eddie about my mega-botany mystery project.

Eddie raised his eyebrows. "Planting a plant? That doesn't sound like a very exciting thing for a superhero to do."

I thought about my plant with no blossoms at home. Eddie was right. It *was* kind of boring.

When we got to class, our math teacher, Mr. Coral, was making a special announcement.

"Students, I have exciting news!" he said. "We are starting a new gardening club, and I would like to invite all of you to join."

"See?" Eddie whispered to me. "Even normal people plant plants."

Mr. Coral continued, "In fact, we are going outside to the school garden to give you a sneak peek at the kind of work we'll be doing in the club."

Can you believe it? Another garden project? It was like my regular life and my superhero life were coming together. This was too strange!

The Normal Elementary School garden was nothing like the greenhouse at the PITS. Sure, it was still full of plants . . . but most of those plants were weeds.

"Okay, class, the main activity today will be weeding," Mr. Coral said. "As soon as the weeds are gone, we can plant some flowers."

Mr. Coral showed us how to pull weeds from the garden and flower boxes.

As it turned out, pulling weeds wasn't fun at all . . . it was hard work! I wished that I could use my superspeed and superstrength. I would have cleared this garden in no time. But I had to keep my superpowers secret. That was part of being a superhero.

I looked over and saw that Eddie wasn't weeding. Instead, he was tinkering with one of his inventions.

"That doesn't look like helping to me," I said.

"Oh yeah? Just watch," said Eddie. "I call this invention the Green Thumb!"

Eddie held up a robotic gardening tool with extendable robot arms that pulled out weeds without harming any other plants. It even watered the plants too!

In case you forgot, Eddie is incredibly smart and invents cool stuff on the spot all the time—his backpack was probably full of spare parts!

The Green Thumb was a hit! It cruised across the garden and schoolyard, picking out weeds while skipping the flowers and other plants.

"Looks like regular school can be just as super as the PITS." Eddie smiled.

And you know what? He was right!

CHAPTER 5

SNIFF!

SNIFF!

PLANT VS. CAT

After school, I ran home to check on my superplant, but what I found was worse than no plant at all.

Chaos was sniffing around my flowerpot again.

"Oh, no you don't," I said as she was about to dig her paws into the dirt.

Of course, Chaos never listened to anybody. But maybe she should have.

Because something happened next that I would never have believed if I hadn't seen it with my own two eyes. A tiny green sprout shot up out of the dirt and wrapped itself around Chaos's paw.

Merp?

Chaos let out a confused sound. She tried to pull her paw away, but another sprout shot up and wrapped itself around another paw, pulling Chaos closer to the pot.

I grabbed hold of Chaos and shouted, "Okay, everybody keep their paws and sprouts to themselves!"

Then just like that, the plant let go.

Chaos jumped from my grasp and bolted into the house. I studied the tiny sprouts. They weren't moving or trying to grab anything. They just looked like pretty normal sprouts.

I was reaching to touch them when Mom surprised me.

"What's gotten into Chaos?" she

asked, and I jumped up like I was the scaredy-cat.

I told her what had happened with the plant.

"Hmm. Chaos has an interesting history with our houseplants," Mom pointed out. "She always ends up destroying them. Like the flowers she pushed off the table. And the hanging plant she used as a swing. Oh, and the parlor palm she used as a hiding place."

I remembered all those moments way too well.

"Those poor plants weren't ready for Chaos," I said.

"No, they weren't." Mom laughed. "But these little sprouts come from superseeds, so maybe Chaos has finally met a plant she can't push around."

Maybe, I thought. But I still wondered what in the world was growing in my backyard.

CHAPTER
6

GUARDING THE GARDEN

That morning, I woke to a strange sound outside. I went to the window and saw Chaos messing with the flowerpot again. I tapped on the glass to get her to stop, when suddenly a GIGANTIC plant sprang up from the pot.

It kept getting bigger and bigger, until it filled up my entire backyard . . . and it was still growing!

"I have to do something before this plant takes over the entire town," I said.

This was definitely a job for MIA MAYHEM! I quick-changed into my suit and flew outside to help.

The plant's vines were lashing the

entire city! I remembered my parents' story about fighting Evil Ivy and Thorn Wrecker. Could the same big bads my parents had battled be back?

I flew toward the vines and used

my superstrength to pull them off buildings like weeds.Then I saw a school bus driving down the street trying to escape the vines, but the vines were too quick. They wrapped around the bus and started to lift it off the ground.

"Not on my watch!" I said as I swooped in to untangle the vines.

The bus was safe, and all the kids cheered. And I gotta say, it felt good to help people.

Also, even though fighting a giant plant was scary, it was also kind of beautiful. After the school bus drove away, I took a moment to admire the massive flowers that lined the street. It was like the entire city was turning into one huge garden.

Then I saw something that I really wasn't expecting. A giant version of Chaos was walking through the city, right toward me!

Chaos let out a meow that was so loud, I covered my ears and closed my eyes.

When I opened them back up, I was in my bed, and everything was back to normal.

Even Chaos was her normal size and being her normal self . . . trying to steal my pillow.

"Phew! It was just a dream!" I said. "But I'd better check my plant, just to make sure."

I ran to my flowerpot, but nothing had changed. There were still only two little sprouts sticking out.

Why won't this plant grow? I wondered.

Then I heard a familiar voice behind me. "Good morning, Mia!"

It was Eddie.

"I saw you run outside and thought you might need some help," he said.

"Maybe I do. I'm worried that my plant isn't growing the way it's supposed to grow," I said. "I planted

my superseeds two days ago, and the only thing that grew were these two tiny sprouts. And they don't seem very super."

"Mind if I take a look?" Eddie asked.

He pinched the soft soil, crumbled it between his fingers, and checked out the sprouts. Luckily, the sprouts didn't try to grab him like they had with Chaos.

"I think I know what's wrong," Eddie

finally said. "This is a case of—"

"Um, a giant monster plant?" I interrupted.

Eddie laughed. "No, I was going to say it's a case of 'be patient.'"

"'Be patient'? What does that mean?" I asked.

"It means plants grow in their own

time," Eddie explained. "And you need to be . . . patient."

You know, Eddie makes a lot of sense sometimes. The plant probably needed more time to grow and bloom, so that's what I would give it. *Still* . . .

"What if it doesn't work?" I asked.

Eddie smiled and pulled out his latest invention. "Then you can borrow the Green Thumb. That way you'll know you did everything right."

CHAPTER
7

TOTALLY NORMAL

I tried my best to take Eddie's advice and be patient with my plant. But being patient is not easy for a kid.

And it's *super* hard when you're a superhero.

A superhero is always ready for action. They're not made to sit around and *wait* for things to happen—which was what I was doing all week.

I woke up every morning and checked on my plant, but nothing changed.

When I got home after school, I went straight to my plant . . . but nothing changed. I even checked again before I went to bed at night . . . still nothing.

I was so nervous. Professor Vine said that our plants should take a week to bloom. And now a week was up!

What if my plant never bloomed? What if I ended up *failing* my mega-botany assignment?

WHOA!

No, that couldn't happen. I had to figure out a way to fix this.

Luckily, on the morning my plant was due back at the PITS, I woke up to find it had transformed! The plant was in full bloom, with purple and green leaves and a tuliplike head. I had never seen anything like it!

I cheered and hugged my plant. Maybe I was totally imagining this, but it kind of felt like the plant was sweetly hugging me *back*.

Hmm, that was strange, I thought.

But I didn't have time to investigate. I had to get to school! So I quickly put the plant and Eddie's Green Thumb into my backpack and rushed off.

Don't ask me how it all fit, but it did.

Hardly anyone at school noticed my plant in my backpack, which was a good thing, because this plant was acting *weird*. The vines kept growing and poking out of my bag. I had to readjust the leaves and vines and then zip them back into my backpack all day.

Maybe Eddie's Green Thumb was making the plant grow so fast. I'd have to tell Eddie that his invention worked a little *too* well.

Finally, the last bell rang, and it was

time to make my way over to the PITS.

I couldn't wait to show what I'd grown to Professor Vine and my friends. But mostly, I was excited to learn what kind of plant it was!

I quick-changed into my supersuit and zoomed to the greenhouse.

Professor Vine wasn't there yet, but Penn and Allie were. Their plants looked great . . . but also, they looked like totally normal plants. Penn had grown a fern, and Allie had grown a raspberry shrub with actual raspberries on its branches.

"Where's your plant, Mia?" Penn asked.

"Um, it's right here," I said.

I slowly unzipped my backpack, and a massive plant thumped out. Had it grown even more during the day?

The plant spread its giant vines in all directions, and its head started to move.

Suddenly the whole class froze and stared at my plant. I wasn't surprised that they were staring. As I looked around the room, I saw that everyone's plants looked totally normal. Everyone's except mine.

"Maybe you grew it wrong," Penn suggested.

I crossed my arms and said, "Impossible! I did everything right."

"Well, your plant looks really . . . weird," Penn said.

"Nonsense! I think it's the most normal plant in the world," I replied.

But then my plant did something completely, absolutely *not* normal. Its vines reached out to grab all the other plants in the greenhouse!

I gulped. "See? Totally normal."

CHAPTER
8

EDDIE'S GREEN THUMB

If anyone ever tells you that plants are boring, don't believe them!

I definitely wouldn't call my plant boring. No, I would describe it more like *out of control*!

Before I knew what was happening, my plant had taken over the entire greenhouse—and it wasn't alone! Because each plant it touched *came to life*!

ARGH!

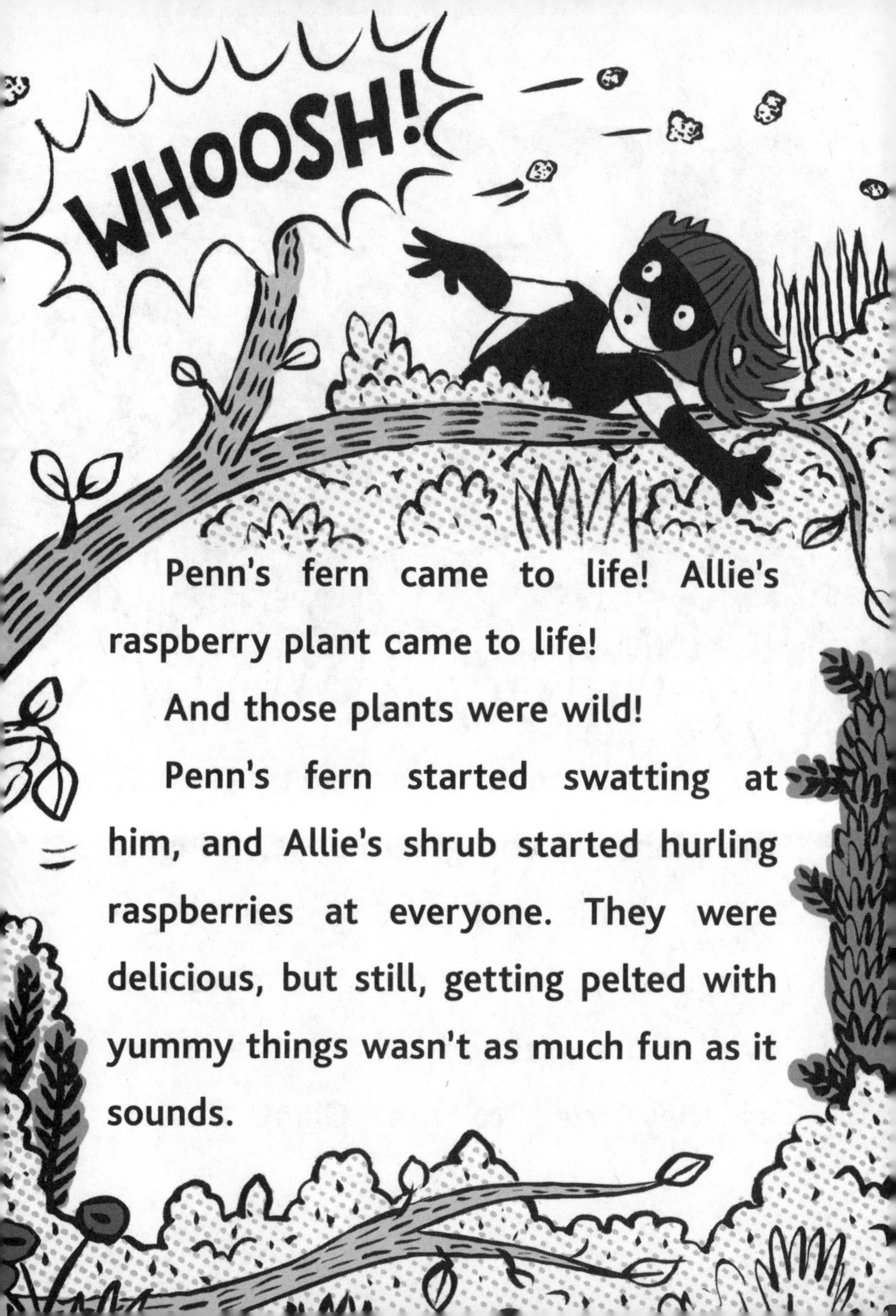

Penn's fern came to life! Allie's raspberry plant came to life!

And those plants were wild!

Penn's fern started swatting at him, and Allie's shrub started hurling raspberries at everyone. They were delicious, but still, getting pelted with yummy things wasn't as much fun as it sounds.

Pretty soon my plant had touched all the plants in the greenhouse, bringing them to life and making them super dangerous! Trees picked up students. Wild roots grabbed kids by the ankles as they tried to run. Giant flowers

leaned over and smelled people . . . and then the flowers *sneezed*! Gross! That made the kids sneeze, which made the flowers sneeze some more, until it was *sneeze-a-palooza* in the greenhouse.

"This is a mess! We've got to do something!" I yelled to my friends. "Allie, can you use your superspeed to run and get Professor Vine?"

"On it!" Allie nodded and took off.

I watched as she darted through a jungle of plants. She ran around a prickly rosebush that suddenly tried to block her path and nearly got lost in a patch of high grass that had grown to be seven feet tall. Then a cluster of poison ivy reached out for her.

"Watch out, Allie!" I yelled.

"Thanks, Mia," Allie called as she swiftly swerved out of the way.

"I wanna help too," said Penn. "What can I do?"

"You're great at flying," I said. "Why don't you get the students out of the trees?"

"Got it!" Penn took flight.

He flew up to the tallest branches and rescued kids like lost kittens or kites. Then he told a funny joke to a Venus flytrap, which, when it laughed, let go of the kids it was trying to capture. Penn caught them all and flew them to safety.

With Penn and Allie hard at work, I knew I also had to do something. I grabbed Eddie's Green Thumb and turned it on. It started snipping and trimming a path through the wild garden. The Green Thumb seemed to be working!

CHAPTER
9

GROWING WILDER

Arrrgh! I spoke too soon!

The plants were growing back, and they were growing wilder than ever! The greenhouse was turning into a jungle.

Maybe it was time to pull weeds like we did in Mr. Coral's gardening club?

So I found the vine closest to me and pulled with all my might. It was *not* easy.

Then the vine grabbed me back and pulled me into a thick tangle of growth. I tried to fly away, but the vine was too strong. Then I heard a very strange voice.

"Mia, it's me . . . your plant."

I looked down and saw that the vine

that held me was attached to my plant. Its bulb opened and closed like a mouth as it spoke to me.

"I'm sorry, Mia. Am I doing something wrong?" the plant asked.

Now, plants don't talk to people every day, but when you're a superhero, you learn to expect the unexpected.

"Um, hi, plant," I said to the plant. "Do you think you could maybe put me down?"

The plant lowered me to the ground.

"Thanks," I said.

"Of course," said the plant. "Is there anything else I can do for you?"

"Well, bringing all the plants to life kinda caused a mess here and scared a lot of people," I pointed out. "Could you ask the other plants to let all the kids go?"

The plant nodded and let out a big breath. *Whoosh!*

It sounded like a gust of wind blowing through the greenhouse. When it was over, all the plants had let the superstudents go.

"Do you want to tell me what's going on?" I asked the plant. "Is this another dream?"

The plant shook its head. "No. This is real. You are not an average superhero, and I am not an average plant."

"That is very clear," I said. "But what kind of plant are you?"

"I can answer that," said Professor Vine as she walked into the greenhouse.

CHAPTER
10

The Frendle Frond

"My, my, my, this is a very special plant you've grown, Mia," Professor Vine said. "It is a Frendle Frond from the X-9 Starfield."

My eyes opened wide with surprise, because it sounded like my plant was truly out of this world.

"Are you telling me that my plant is from another planet?" I asked.

"Try another solar system," said Professor Vine. "I'm sorry, Mia. I'm not sure how these superseeds made it to you, but you've done an amazing job with your plant. Frendle Fronds are wonderful in gardens because they can

speak directly to other plants to help them grow. But sometimes they can get too excited."

"Oh, plant shoots!" said the Frendle Frond. "Did I go a little overboard?"

"Well, on Earth, we don't grow our gardens to be theme parks with plants as adventure rides," Professor Vine said. "In fact, we don't ride them at all! We appreciate their natural beauty."

I nodded. "Frendle, do you think you could use *your* superpower to help calm the garden? All the other students worked hard to grow their plants, and it would be great to let them show off their cool projects."

"Sure thing, Mia," said the Frendle Frond.

The giant plant started humming as it turned the garden back to normal.

The PITS greenhouse was in full bloom with beautiful and *calm* plants once again. Everyone cheered, and the Frendle Frond took a bow.

All my classmates presented their plants and then planted them in the greenhouse . . . with the Frendle Frond's help, of course.

Right before class was over, the Frendle Frond returned Eddie's Green Thumb to me.

"I believe this is yours," the plant said. "Thank you for such a wonderful invention. It helped me grow by removing weeds and other things that can be harmful to plants in a garden."

I couldn't wait to tell Eddie what the Frendle Frond had said about his Green Thumb. Oh, and I thought I should tell him about this whole wild adventure, too.

But as I left the PITS and headed back home, I had a sneaky feeling that I was forgetting something.

Oh well. I shrugged. *I'm sure I'll remember it if it's important. . . .*